Lorraine

The GIRL who SANG the STORM AWAY

sourcebooks
jabberwocky

written by Ketch Secor

illustrated by Higgins Bond

Sourcebooks and the colophon are registered trademarks of Sourcebooks, Inc.

The final art was rendered in acrylic paint.

Published by Sourcebooks Jabberwocky, an imprint of Sourcebooks, Inc.
P.O. Box 4410, Naperville, Illinois 60567-4410
(630) 961-3900
Fax: (630) 961-2168
sourcebooks.com

Library of Congress Cataloging-in-Publication Data

Names: Secor, Ketch, author. | Bond, Higgins, illustrator.
Title: Lorraine / Ketch Secor, [Higgins Bond].
Description: Naperville, Illinois : Sourcebooks Jabberwocky, [2018] |
  Summary: Pa Paw and Lorraine always lift their spirits by playing music
  together, but their instruments are missing when a fearsome storm hits the
  Tennessee hills.
Identifiers: LCCN 2016058178 | (13 : alk. paper)
Subjects: | CYAC: Stories in rhyme. | Music--Fiction. |
  Grandfathers--Fiction. | Crows--Fiction. | Storms--Fiction.
Classification: LCC PZ7.1.S33694 Lor 2018 | DDC [E]--dc23 LC record available at https://lccn.loc.gov/2016058178

Source of Production: PrintPlus Limited, Shenzhen, Guangdong Province, China
Date of Production: June 2018
Run Number: 5012429

Printed and bound in China.
PP 10 9 8 7 6 5 4 3 2 1

For Lydia.

—KETCH SECOR

For my beautiful grandchildren:
Andrew, Alexis, and Annabella.
May they always keep music in their hearts.

—HIGGINS BOND

ON A TENNESSEE FARM

where the music grows wild

lived a pitchforkin' Pa Paw
and his fearless grandchild.

Snakes didn't scare her and neither did spiders.
Lorraine had a cartload of COURAGE inside her.

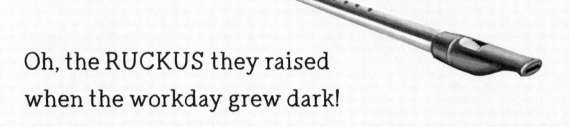

Oh, the RUCKUS they raised
when the workday grew dark!

With Lorraine on her whistle
and Pa Paw on his harp.

The songs they sang always lifted their spirits—
on good days or bad it was JOYFUL to hear it.

And even when storms hit those Tennessee hills,

the music they played
made their worries stand still.

One morning they played 'neath the Chinkypin tree,
when—BY JINGO!—a crow landed right at their feet.

"Look, Pa Paw! HE DANCES!

Let's play it again!"

Well, by the last chorus,
she'd found A TRUE FRIEND.

But one day at breakfast, Lorraine thought,

"That's weird—

the
bright,

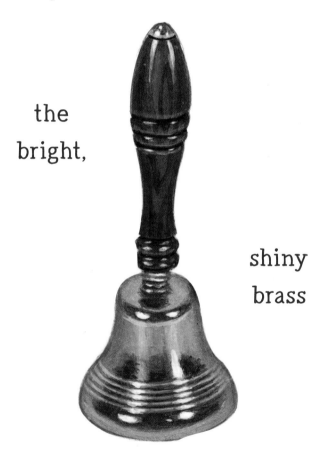

shiny
brass

dinner bell disappeared."

And out in the pigpen
she noticed something STRANGE:
the tin scoop was missing
from the bin full of grain.

Then the keys simply vanished
from poor Pa Paw's pocket.
When he went to the barn gate,
he couldn't unlock it.

Soon all of the shiniest things in the place

were gone!
Pinched!
Lifted!
Without any trace!

"IT'S A THIEF," said Lorraine,
and he's gone on a spree!"
"By gum!" wondered Pa Paw.
"Just who could it be?"

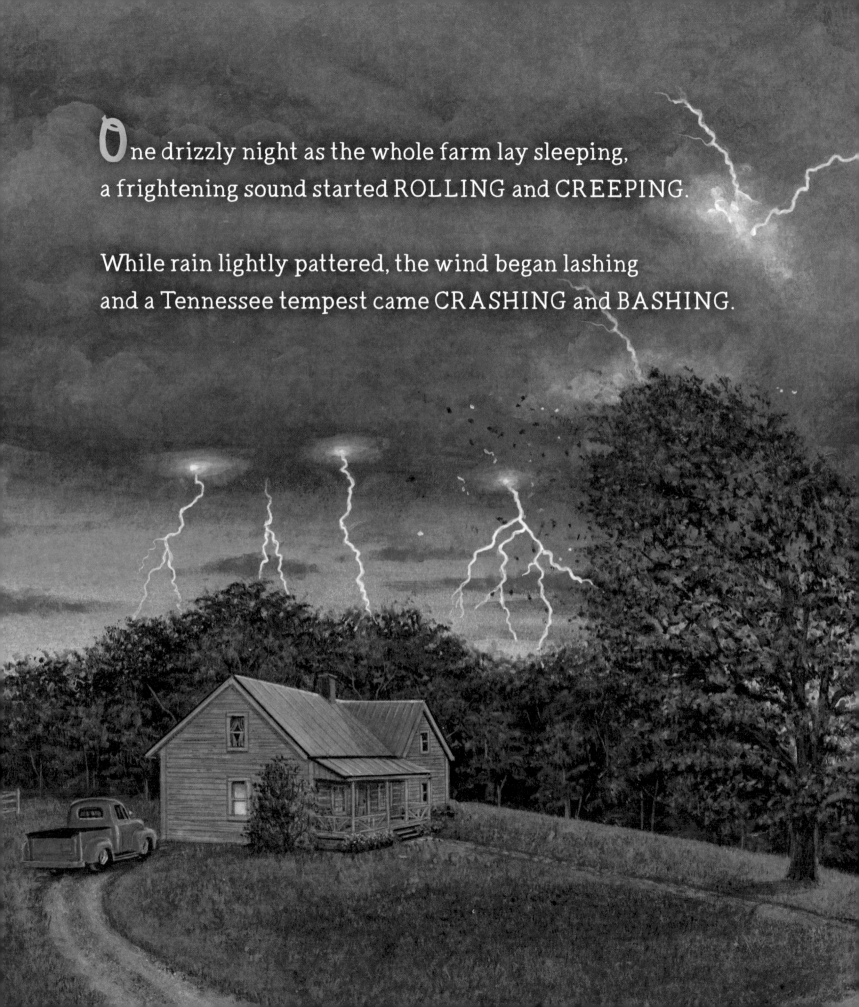

One drizzly night as the whole farm lay sleeping,
a frightening sound started ROLLING and CREEPING.

While rain lightly pattered, the wind began lashing
and a Tennessee tempest came CRASHING and BASHING.

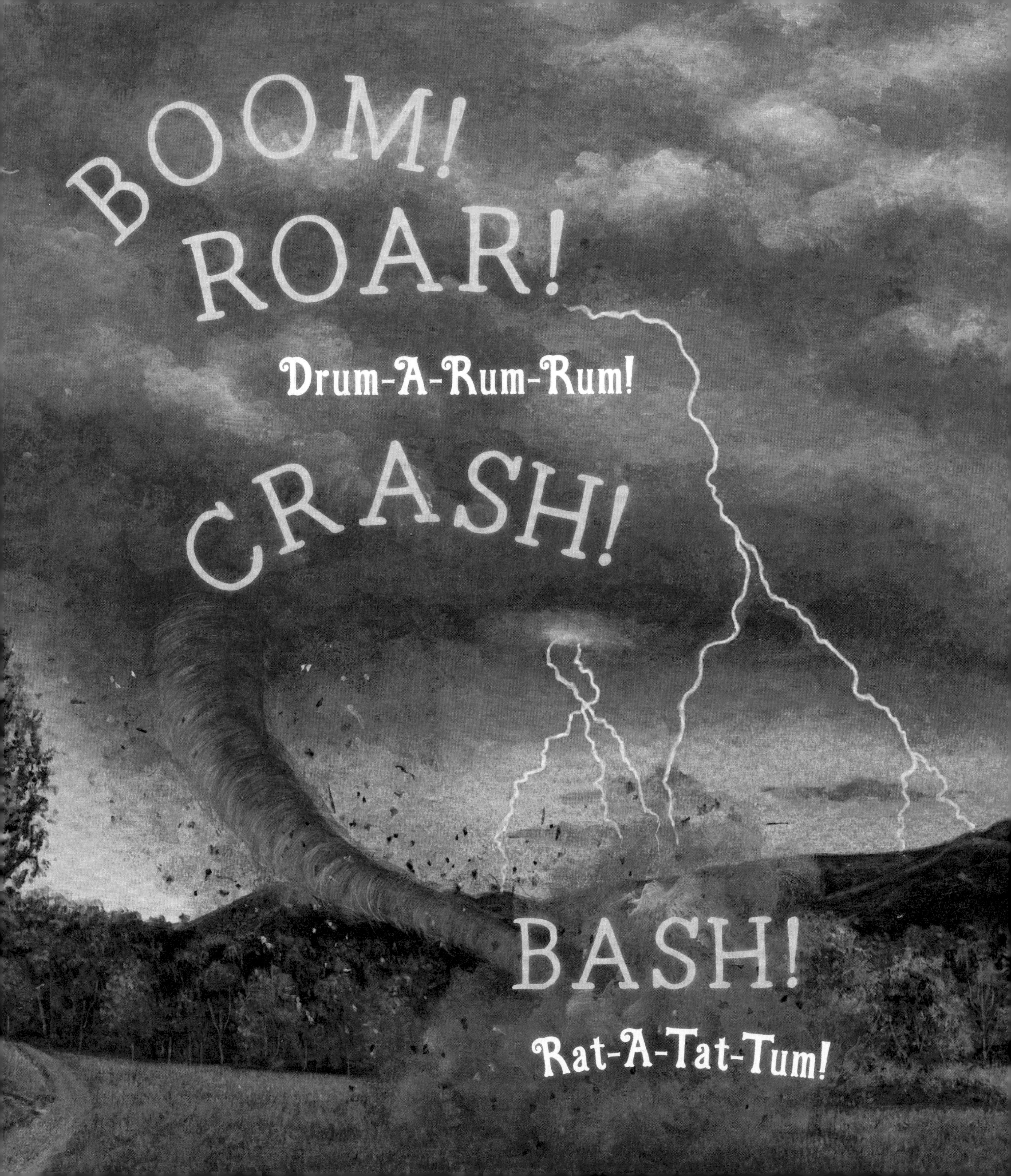
BOOM!
ROAR!
Drum-A-Rum-Rum!
CRASH!
BASH!
Rat-A-Tat-Tum!

"Oh, Pa Paw! The storm must be right overhead.
I'm fearful!
I'm frightened!
I'm all full of dread!

There's only ONE WAY we can ride out this thunder.

I'll go get my whistle.
Let's knock out a number."

So Pa Paw reached in where his French harp was kept.
"BY GUM!" he said. "I've been harmonica-napped!"

Then Lorraine looked around,
but her eyes filled with tears.
"My pennywhistle's gone! I've had it nine years!"

But old, smiling Pa Paw, he hugged her in tight.
"Now, listen, Lorraine, we'll get through this night.

See, a twister can frighten with whirling black wind,
and a rainstorm makes landslides and flash floods begin.

A tempest could tear this whole homeplace apart,
but it can't touch the music
that's deep in your heart!"

"Child, you ALWAYS made music when you were afraid, and sadly your instrument's stolen away.

But who NEEDS a whistle
or some SHINY thing

when you've got a voice
and a song you can sing!"

Then out from her room,
she COURAGEOUSLY crept.

"Oh, Pa Paw, you're right!
No, we're sure NOT licked yet!"

Then Lorraine sang up HIGH,
and old Pa Paw sang LOW,

and they STOMPED and they STAMPED
with a **BIG** do-si-do.

Singing

"Fire on the Mountain"

and "Pig in the Pen,"

"Shortnin' Bread,"

"Shout Lula,"

"Geese in the Glen."

Oh, they sang and they shouted 'til the first light of day,

and their song chased that storm
and their worries away.

Quick from the window

came Pa Paw's voice calling,

"The Chinkypin tree in the front yard has fallen!

"LOOK!" stuttered Pa Paw.
"Do you see what's inside?"

"EVERYTHING MISSING!" said Lorraine with surprise.

For deep in the heart
of the smoldering tree,
lay a trove FULL OF TREASURES
that shined silvery.

Pa Paw reached into the dark hiding place,
and a smile lit up in his weathered old face.

For tucked in a hollow stuffed with
weeds, straw, and thistle,

he found
his French harp

and **Lorraine's pennywhistle.**

They broke into song with their hearts all aglow,
when "CAW, CAW, CAW," came the voice of the crow!
He was perched on the stump of the old Chinkypin,
dancing a jig with a mischievous grin.

How their HAPPY eyes shone
as they danced to the tune
and they planted a Chinkypin seedling to bloom.

Then the clouds parted ways as
the music rose high,

and the SUNSHINE SPARKLED
in the Tennessee sky.

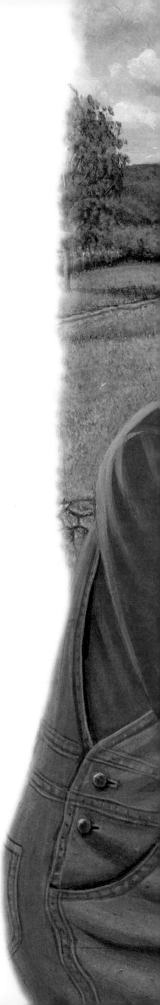